D1032347

SESAME STREET 123

TO:

_____

_____

FROM:

_____

_____

123 SESAME STREET

STORYBOOK COLLECTION
Treasury of Love

sourcebooks
wonderland

Sesame Street is a place full of laughter and learning. Since 1969, the show has reached children around the world through its lovable characters and educational content. It's a place where all children can explore and play and grow and share. With the help of Elmo, Cookie Monster, and other friends, preschoolers are growing up smarter, stronger, and kinder.

In the hearts of millions of children and adults—and in more than 150 countries around the globe—Sesame Street continues to create a brighter, better place for us all.

We celebrate love, kindness, perseverance, individuality, and dreaming big with this special book that shows the values of Sesame Street can be found everywhere.

Table of Contents

LOVE is dancing by yourself to your favorite song.

LOVE

IS BEING AN EVERYDAY

HERO.

LOVE
IS INFINITE—
BIGGER THAN ALL OF
THE NUMBERS.

comes in all
SHAPES and SIZEs.

is building something together.

LOVE

IS GIGGLES,
AND KISSES, AND HUGS,
AND SQUISHES.

LOVE SINGS IN EVERY LANGUAGE.

LOVE
is being kind to all
your best friends.

MAKES
ALL
KINDS
OF
SOUNDS.

HONK, HONK!

LOVE

IS ACCEPTING
LIFE EVEN WHEN
IT IS MESSY!

 **is**

  and a soft bunny.

is

cookies...
and then
more cookies.

LOVE is magical and full of WONDER.

Love is everywhere

and all around us.

Love

Find the hearts!

Go back through the story and see if you can find a heart hidden on these pages!

- ♥ **Love is a sunny day!**
- ♥ **Love is infinite—bigger than all of the numbers.**
- ♥ Love is being kind to all your best friends.
- ♥ **Love is accepting life even when it is messy!**
- ♥ **Love is an amazing family and a soft bunny.**
- ♥ Love is everywhere and all around us.

Kindness MAKES THE WORLD GO ROUND

By Craig Manning

Illustrated by Joe Mathieu

Elmo woke up to a bright, cheery sun.
The day was brand new. He was ready for fun!

It wasn't his birthday, but there on the floor,
was a gift wrapped in paper and ribbons galore.

to Elmo

Inside was a camera, and attached was a note.
It was from Elmo's mommy, and on it she wrote:

"Here's a gift for my boy, and there is a reason—
though it's not your birthday or the holiday season.

"It's World Kindness Day, a day to show caring,
a day to be thoughtful, for giving and sharing.

"I'm giving to you, for you're sweeter than sweet.
Now go capture kindness on Sesame Street!"

Elmo looked all around, then a thought came to mind:
"What kinds of kindness might Elmo soon find?

Those who are friendly or thoughtful or giving?"
He wanted to go see where kindness was living.

All through the day, Elmo learned many things,
like how Big Bird showed kindness with just his two wings:
holding the door for friends half his size…
or perhaps even smaller—they're such tiny guys!

The best gifts are ones that are given with love,
be they cameras or flowers or old baseball gloves.

The thought is what counts at the end of the day—
even if grouches don't like rose bouquets.

Elmo learned something simple, like sharing a sweater
can brighten a day and make the world better.

That kindness is not just about what we show
to friends that we love, or to people we know.

Kindness is something we can give everyone—
every person or thing that lives under the sun,
from the birds in the sky to the worms in the ground.
Kindness is what makes the world go around.

Elmo photographed Cookie—the flash was so bright!—
and remembered the value of being polite.

No matter the monster, no matter the place,
to say "please" and then "thank you" will always show grace.

Elmo learned that a friend always offers a hand
to help someone up when he cannot stand.

And even if *you* end up falling down too,
it's still right to put someone else before you!

Elmo captured a message that everyone knows:
"Sharing is caring," as the old saying goes!

Rosita and Zoe know the best thing to do
is not to eat ice cream with one spoon, but two!

Elmo noticed some kindness is shown with a broom,
or by raking the leaves, or by cleaning your room!

Kindness takes practice, but when you deliver,
you may be surprised—it's great being the GIVER!

Elmo stopped at the park. He had finished his quest.
His mom had been right—being kind was the best!

As Elmo and Julia took turns on the slide,
the little red monster felt all warm inside.

Back home with his photos, Elmo sat down
and thought of the things that he'd seen around town.

The generous spirit of family and friends
showed him the best way to mark the day's end.

When his mother came home a bit later that night,
a hug from her Elmo made all the world bright.

He gave her a gift tied with red bows galore,
and she opened it up as they sat on the floor.

The gift was a scrapbook, with a note on page one
that read "Happy Kindness Day, with love from your son!"

They flipped through the photos; together they found
that kindness is what makes the world go around.

a little
book about
the BIG POWER
of PERSEVERANCE

YOU CAN DO IT!

SESAME STREET

sourcebooks
wonderland

By Craig Manning
Illustrated by Joe Mathieu

Elmo was learning to write his own name,
but the harder he tried, the worse it became!
Is it L before M, or M before L?
Elmo mixed up the letters and he just couldn't tell.

"Elmo gives up!" Elmo cried, feeling helpless and sad.
He was frustrated and also a little bit mad!
"You can do it! Don't give up!" said his mom from the door.
"With a mind made for growing, you can always learn more."

"You learned how to crawl, then you learned how to walk!
You learned how to sing once you learned how to talk.
You learned how to ride your very own trike,
and one day you'll learn how to ride a big bike!"

"It wasn't easy, but still you learned how.
You didn't give up, and look at you now!"

She's right, Elmo thought, and he knew what to do.
He'd practice and practice, then he'd write his name too!

Elmo did it! He wrote his name down nice and neat!
But how 'bout his friends around Sesame Street?
Were there things they were trying to learn how to do?
Who else could use some encouragement too?

"Skating's too hard!" Grover said with a sigh.
He sat on the curb and he started to cry!

"You can do it!" said Elmo. "With a hand from a friend, you can skate on the sidewalk from beginning to end!"

What was the Count making? Could Grover guess?
"Of course not," Count cried. "It looks like a mess!"

"You can do it!" said Grover. "Keep painting away. Practice makes perfect—you will get it someday!"

Cookie Monster loved cookies, the eating and baking,
but he struggled a lot with the counting and waiting.

"You can do it!" said Count. This is something Count knows.
"Now here's a quick tip—use your fingers and toes!"

Telly loved triangles—they were the best!
But when it came to new shapes, he forgot all the rest.

"You can do it!" said Cookie. "Me thinks you'll be great. Just look at circles as cookies or plates!"

While playing with Rosita, Abby started to pout.
She kept dropping the ball and she wanted to shout!

"You can do it!" said Telly. "Just try not to stress.
Take in a big breath and try worrying less!"

Julia loved dancing—she spun really well.
But then she tried leaping, and whoops!—almost fell.

"You can do it!" said Abby. "You'll shine bright like the sun! You don't need to be perfect! You just need to have fun!"

Zoe was hoping to play, skip, and run,
but she couldn't keep going with her laces undone.

"You can do it!" said Julia. "You'll tie a knot and a bow!"
Keep training your fingers and you'll be a pro!

Riding a bike was Big Bird's big dream,
which is easier said than done, it would seem!

"You can do it!" said Zoe. "It's okay to fall!
Just get back up, and watch out for that wall!"

So what thing do *you* want to learn how to do?
Is it running or singing or tying your shoes?
Because if Grover can skate, and Elmo can write,
and Julia can leap in a big, bright spotlight…

If Telly learned shapes, and Abby caught a ball,
and Cookie, Count, Zoe, and Big Bird did it all...

then you're the next learner! So go on, get going!
***You* can do it**, my friend! Don't ever stop growing!

You CAN DO IT!

You CAN do whatever you set your mind to if you just keep trying!

Each day, tell yourself:

I am smart.

I am strong.

I am kind.

I am brave.

I am helpful.

I am unique.

I can learn new things.

I can do anything!

JUST ONE YOU!

By Lillian Jaine
Illustrated by Joe Mathieu

SESAME STREET

sourcebooks
wonderland

This is a story that's all about you,
and all the **spectacular** things that you do.

So please come along and we'll show you it's true—
there is just one and only wonderful YOU!

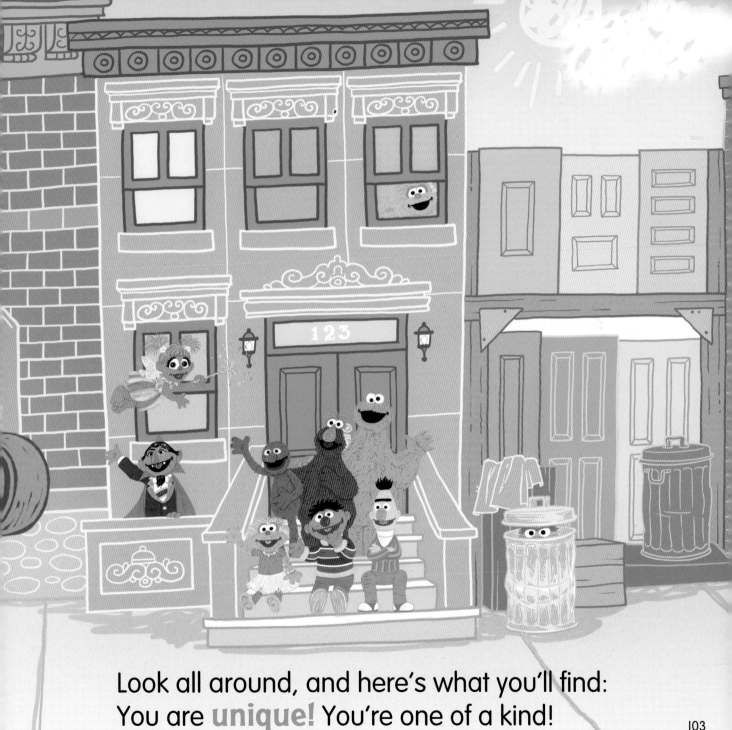

Look all around, and here's what you'll find:
You are **unique!** You're one of a kind!

The **smile** on your face is like no smile I've seen.
You're one special person, if you know what I mean.

Your mind's full of **magic** to thrill and delight!
Even on dark days, you make the world bright!

No job is too **big**; no task is too **small**.
No matter what comes, you tackle it all!

You're strong and you're brave;
you're a grand **superhero**.
You give one hundred percent;
you never give zero!

You dance and you **dream**
from dusk until dawn.
Don't ever stop trying!
We'll cheer you on!

Your **adventures** may take you
away from your home,
but your best friends will be there
wherever you roam.

Everyone knows how terrific you are.
We've always been sure that you will go **far!**

Because even if something doesn't quite go your way,

you will turn things **around** the very next day!

You're **perfect** as you—there's no one who's better!
So be true to yourself, and always remember…

There is just **one** you.
No other person does the things that you do.

Yes, it's absolutely, positively true.
There's just one and only wonderful **you!**

Be Proud of

Just One You

Dream

with Sesame Street

By Susanna Leonard Hill

Illustrated by Marybeth Nelson

A dream can be big or a dream can be small.

What matters the most is to have dreams at all.

Ambitious, creative, outrageous, concrete,

or close to your heart, something simple and sweet.

A dream can be near or a dream can be far.

It even can push you to reach for the stars.

Wherever you go, way up to new heights,

if you keep trying, your dreams will take flight!

Though beginning seems hard with no ending in sight,

each story begins with the first word you write.

A single note starts the most beautiful song.

One step gets your dream up and moving along.

When things don't work out in just the right ways,

remember you grow when you get through bad days.

Don't be scared of a monster hiding on the next page.

Keep learning, keep dreaming, no matter your age!

Since one person's trash is another one's treasure,

your dreams are not subject to anyone's measure.

Even if others may not think it's best,

the road to success is your own special quest.

It's perfectly fine to do things your own way.

However you do them, it's always okay.

How boring if everyone did things the same.

So imagine! Have fun! And play your own game!

Sometimes big ideas don't go as you planned.

Giant leaps lead to stumbles and falls when you land.

But pick yourself up. Try again the next day.

Get back on that stage—everything's A-OK!

A wand isn't needed to make dreams come true.

The magic you need is already in you!

Forget about fairy dust, potions, and spells.

You've got all you need to succeed and excel!

If your dream is too big to complete on your own,

teamwork is better than working alone.

You always can ask a good friend for advice,

and working together sure does feel nice!

If you're worried about making a lot of mistakes,

and wondering whether you have what it takes,

remember you don't need a superhero's cape!

Just believe in yourself and your dreams will take shape.

Though you're sure to have days when you can't try a smile,

look on the sweet side of life for a while.

Cookies and milk sweep the gray clouds away

and bring you right back to a bright sunny day.

Some dreams you will hold very close to your heart

but others are better when friends can take part.

If your dream seems as if it will never come true,

keep in mind you're surrounded by those who love you.

You're amazing and smart in all that you do.

Count your blessings for all that is given to you.

Make every day count to achieve something new.

Every day is a chance for a dream to come true.

Although you work hard toward your dreams every day,

make sure you take time out to giggle and play.

Be happy. Be silly. Make a funny face!

Reaching your dreams is not some big race.

155

When one dream is realized, the next can shine through,

pushing you forward to try something new.

Never stop dreaming, whatever you do.

Here's wishing that all of your dreams will come true!

Dreams are amazing.

Dreams are magical.

What is your **dream?**

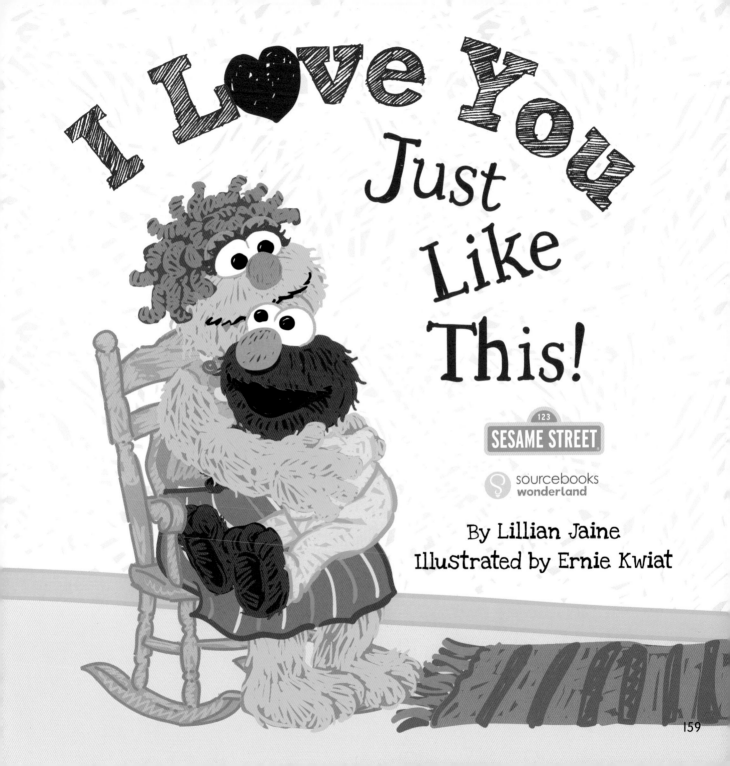

I L♥ve You Just Like This!

SESAME STREET

sourcebooks wonderland

By Lillian Jaine

Illustrated by Ernie Kwiat

Elmo and his mommy
were talking late one night,
snuggled up together,
cozy, warm, and tight.

"I love you, Mommy,"
Elmo whispered in her ear.
Elmo's mommy smiled.
"I love you too, my dear."

"I've loved you all your life,
every single day.
I love you oh so much—
I'll tell you all the ways!"

I love you brighter
than **1** sun up in the sky.

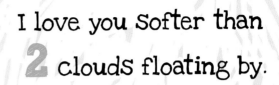

I love you softer than **2** clouds floating by.

I love you sweeter than **3** crunchy, yummy treats.

I love you bigger than **4** giant, hairy feet!

I love you spookier than **5** big flying bats.

I love you taller
than **6** tall, towering hats.

I love you more than the
number **7**, **8**, or **9**.

I love you more than **1** through **10** combined!

I love you from your **head**
all the way down to your **toes**.

I love your silly **laugh**,
your **smile**,
and your **nose**.

I love you **redder** than the nicest, reddest rose.

I love you **bluer** than Cookie Monster's toes!

I'd love you if you were **big**

or very, very **small**.

174

I'd love you if you were **short**
or really, really **tall**!

I love you when you're messy.
I love you when you're **NEAT**.

I love you when you're **grouchy**
(and even more when you are **sweet**).

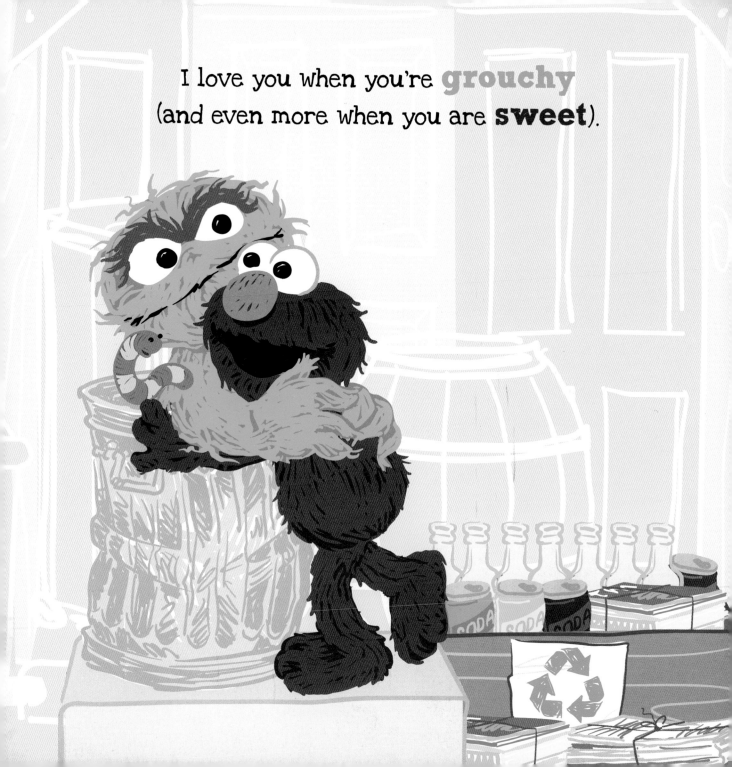

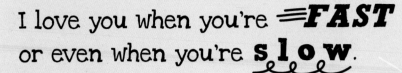

I love you when you're *FAST*
or even when you're **slow**.

178

I love you **more**
than you will ever really know.

I love you **higher** than a hero in the sky.

I love you **deeper**
than the river
rushing by.

I always love you
on a bright and **sunny** day.

I also love you
when the **rain** won't go away.

I love to be with you through
seasons one and all.

I love you all the flowers of **spring**
and all the leaves of **fall**.

I love you when you're **near**;
I love you when you're **far**.

I love you **all the time**,
no matter where you are!

I love you often, always,
  and time and time again.
I love you from the beginning
  to the very end.

Now I'll give you a hug,
  and you give me a kiss.
And don't ever forget,

I love you just like this.

Cover and internal design copyright © 2021 by Sourcebooks
Cover illustrations copyright © Sesame Workshop
Text by Craig Manning, Lillian Jaine, Susanna Leonard Hill
Illustrations by Ernie Kwiat, Joe Mathieu, Marybeth Nelson

Sourcebooks and the colophon are registered trademarks of Sourcebooks.
All rights reserved.

The characters and events portrayed in this book are fictitious or are used fictitiously.
Any similarity to real persons, living or dead, is purely coincidental and not intended by the author.
Published by Sourcebooks Wonderland, an imprint of Sourcebooks Kids

P.O. Box 4410, Naperville, Illinois 60567–4410
(630) 961-3900
sourcebookskids.com
Source of Production: Hung Hing Off-Set Printing Co. Ltd.,
Shenzhen, Guangdong Province, China
Date of Production: June 2021
Run Number: 5022036

Printed and bound in China.
HH 10 9 8 7 6 5 4 3 2 1